Ellin ✓ W9-DGN-973

PEGGY PARISH

THE CATS' BURGLAR

pictures by
LYNN SWEAT

A Young Yearling Book

Published by
Dell Publishing
a division of
The Bantam Doubleday Dell Publishing Group, Inc.
666 Fifth Avenue
New York, New York 10103

Text copyright © 1983 by Margaret Parish
Illustrations copyright © 1983 by Lynn Sweat

All rights reserved. No part of this book may be reproduced or trans-
mitted in any form or by any means, electronic or mechanical, includ-
ing photocopying, recording, or by any information storage and re-
trieval system, without the written permission of the Publisher, except
where permitted by law. For information address: Greenwillow Books,
a division of William Morrow & Company, Inc., New York, New York.

The trademark Yearling® is registered in the U.S. Patent
and Trademark Office.

ISBN: 0-440-40054-6

Reprinted by arrangement with Greenwillow Books, a division of
William Morrow & Company, Inc.

Printed in the United States of America

May 1988

10 9 8 7 6 5 4 3 2

W

For Ada's Sally, Sweeper, and Peggy,
for Susie's Krispy,
and for all of my cats —
past, present and future —
with love

"Oh, Aunt Emma,"
said Mrs. James.
"Not another cat!"
"Isn't he cute?"
said Aunt Emma.
"I named him Baby Bear."

Mr. James looked around.
Cats were here, there,
everywhere.
"Look at them," he said.
"They are tearing
up everything."

"I don't care,"

  said Aunt Emma.

"Everything is old anyway.

  I love to see them play.

  They make me laugh."

"You have too many cats,"

  said Miss Wilson.

"We worry about you.

  People are laughing at you."

"Oh, shush," said Aunt Emma.

"I'm an old lady.

I don't care what people say."

She looked at the clock.

"My goodness," she said.

"It is my bedtime.

All of you, shoo."

Aunt Emma's friends left.

"I will see you tomorrow,"
she called.

"Have a good night,"
called Mr. James.

Aunt Emma looked around.
Cats were here, there,
everywhere.

She laughed and said,

"I do have a lot.

But I like cats."

Aunt Emma went
into her bedroom.
The cats followed her.

Aunt Emma got ready for bed.

"Are you all here?" she said.

"I see one, two, three, four,
five, six, seven–"

Aunt Emma looked all around.

"Bunny, Muffy," she called.

"Where are you?"

Bump! Bump! Bump!

"Oh, oh," said Aunt Emma.

"They are shut up."

She followed the bumps.

"The closet!" she said.

She opened the closet door.

Bunny and Muffy ran out.

"I'm sorry," said Aunt Emma.

"I must be more careful."

Aunt Emma got into bed.

"Good night, cats," she said.

The cats lay down here,

there, everywhere.

Soon everyone was asleep.

Aunt Emma stayed asleep.

But the cats did not.

One by one they woke up.

They began to play.

They raced through the house.

But Aunt Emma did not

hear them.

Then suddenly, cats jumped
onto her bed.

Aunt Emma did wake up.

She sat up.

"What-what!" she said.

The cats were very quiet.

They listened.

Aunt Emma listened, too.

She heard a noise.

She did not know
what made the noise.

Then she heard another noise.

ACHOO!

She knew what made that noise.

"Oh, my goodness!"

said Aunt Emma.

"Someone is in my house."

Quietly she got up.
Quietly she closed
her bedroom door.
She locked it.

Aunt Emma called the police.

"This is Aunt Emma,"

she said.

"A burglar is in my house."

"We will come right over,"

said Chief Dan.

Aunt Emma hung up

the telephone.

"Thank you, cats," she said.

"Are you all here?"

She put on her light.
"One, two, three, four,
five, six, seven, eight,"
she counted.
"Someone is missing."
She looked at the cats.

"Baby Bear!" said Aunt Emma.

She looked around the room.

There was no Baby Bear.

"What should I do?"

said Aunt Emma.

ACHOO!

The cats jumped.

Aunt Emma jumped, too.

"Burglar or not," she said,

"I must find Baby Bear."

Quietly she opened her door.

Quietly she walked out.

Quietly the cats followed.

Aunt Emma saw a dim light.

She saw a burglar.

And she saw Baby Bear.

"*Achoo!* Go away, cat!"

said the burglar.

"*Achoo!* Go away!"

Baby Bear wanted to play.

He wanted the burglar to play.

Aunt Emma smiled.

She put on the light.

The burglar jumped.

Baby Bear jumped, too.

He jumped on the burglar's leg.

"Ouch! *Achoo!*" said the burglar.

"*Achoo!* Get down! *Achoo!*"

Aunt Emma stared.

She stared at the burglar.

"Oh, my goodness!"

she said.

Scruffy stared, too.

The burglar wore a hat.

The hat had a feather.

Scruffy wanted that feather.

He took a big jump.

He landed on the burglar.

And Scruffy got that feather.

"*Achoo! Achoo!* Help!"

yelled the burglar.

"*Achoo!* Save me! *Achoo!*"

36

Scooter hated yelling.

She arched her back.

She hissed.

She spat.

This scared Muffy.

It scared Puff.

They wanted to hide.

They saw the burglar's bag.

It was open.

Muffy and Puff jumped in.

CRASH!

The bag fell to the floor.

Bunny and Bunkins jumped.

They jumped on the burglar.

Judy Trudy followed them.

"*Achoo!* Please, lady,"

said the burglar.

"Please-*achoo*-help me!

Cats-*achoo*-make-*achoo*-

me sneeze."

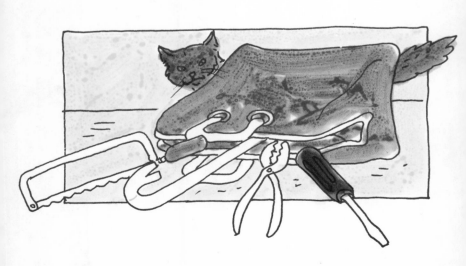

Just then Nicky jumped
on the burglar's head.
"*ACHOO!*" sneezed the burglar.
"Get them off! *Achoo!*
I can't-*achoo*-move."

But the burglar did move.

He began to shake.

The cats clung to him.

They were having fun.

"*Achoo!* Stop!"
yelled the burglar.
"They are–*achoo*–hurting me."

Aunt Emma's eyes began to twinkle.

"All right, cats," she said.

"Don't be greedy.

Just take little bites.

There is enough of him

for all of you."

"Oh, no! *Achoo!*"
yelled the burglar.
"You are a witch!"
"And you are a burglar,"
said Aunt Emma.
"That is not nice."

"Please—*achoo*—please,"

said the burglar.

"Please—*achoo*—let me go."

"Oh, no," said Aunt Emma.

"I can't do that.

My cats like you."

The cats ran around him.

They jumped on him.

They jumped over him.

"*Achoo!*" cried the burglar.

Aunt Emma tried not to laugh.

But she had to.

"RRRRRRRRR,"

screamed the sirens.

"RRRrrrrr."

Aunt Emma ran to open the door.

The cats ran to hide.

Policemen ran into the house.

"Aunt Emma!" said Chief Dan.

"Are you all right?"

Aunt Emma nodded her head.

She couldn't talk.

She was laughing too hard.

"Help! *Achoo!*"

yelled the burglar.

"Please–*achoo*–save me

from these cats."

The policemen looked around.

"Cats?" said Chief Dan.

"What cats?"

The burglar looked around.

He saw no cats.

"But–but," he said,

"they were–*achoo*–here.

There–*achoo*–were lots of them."

Meow.

Chief Dan looked down.

There was Baby Bear.

Chief Dan picked him up.

Baby Bear began to purr.

"This little kitten scared you?"
said Chief Dan.

"Take him—*achoo*—away,"
yelled the burglar.

"*Achoo! Achoo! Achoo!*"

Everybody laughed.

Scooter walked up
to the burglar.
She hissed at him.

Then cats popped out
here, there, everywhere.

"*Achoo!* Please save me!"

yelled the burglar.

"I will-*achoo*-never-*achoo*-

steal again."

Aunt Emma laughed.

"That was so funny," she said.

"No," said Chief Dan.

"Burglars are never funny."

"You are right," said Aunt Emma.

"I was very lucky,

my cats saved me."

"Thank you, cats," Chief Dan said.

He took the burglar away.

The next day,
all of the neighbors came
to visit.
"Now what do you think?"
said Aunt Emma.
"Do I have too many cats?"
"Indeed not!" said Mr. James.

"Aunt Emma! Aunt Emma!"
yelled Mary and Don.
They came running.
"Look what we found,"
said Mary.
"Oh, what a cute kitten,"
said Aunt Emma.

"Will you take it?" said Don.

The neighbors began to laugh.

But Aunt Emma

held out her hands.

"Of course I will," she said.